FARAWAY FAMILIES

By Betsy Loredo

Illustrated by
Monisha Raja

SILVER MOON PRESS
New York

First Silver Moon Press Edition 1995

For information contact:
Silver Moon Press
126 Fifth Avenue
Suite 803
New York, NY 10011
(800) 874-3320

Design: John J. H. Kim

Library of Congress Cataloging-in-Publication Data

Loredo, Betsy, 1963-
Faraway families /by Betsy Loredo;
[illustrated by Monisha Raja]. – 1st ed.
p. cm. – (Family ties)
ISBN 1-881889-61-0: $12.95
1.Family–United States–Juvenile literature.
2. Family–United States–Case studies–Juvenile literature.
3. Separation (psychology)–Juvenile literature.
[1. Family life. 2. Separation (psychology)]
I. Raja, Monisha, ill. II. Title. III. Series: Family ties (New York, NY) .
HQ536.L67 1994
306.85\0973–dc20
94-22978
CIP AC
10 9 8 7 6 5 4 3 2 1
Printed in the USA

Table of Contents

INTRODUCTION
MILES APART.. 1

CHAPTER ONE
WHEN WE'RE APART 3

CHAPTER TWO
SHOWING YOU CARE..............................13

CHAPTER THREE
WILL YOU REMEMBER ME?.....................21

CHAPTER FOUR
FAMILY PHOTOS 29

CHAPTER FIVE
WHAT'S NEW? EVERYTHING!....................38

ACTIVITIES
YOUR FAMILY TREE................................48
SHOW-YOU-CARE PACKAGE 53

GLOSSARY 55

V

Introduction

MILES APART

Felicia lives in one town, but her grandparents live in different towns far away. Josh has aunts, uncles, and cousins spread clear across the country. Stacey even has family scattered around the world!

Does that sound familiar? Does it sound like your family?

Not all families can live in one place. Members of the family take jobs in other cities, get married and relocate, or go to school out of state. Grandparents and cousins may be miles away. And even a parent, sister, or brother sometimes has to live far away.

It's not easy being separated from someone you love. You may feel lonely, afraid, sad, even angry. You might

 wonder: Does he miss me as much as I miss him? What is she doing right now? What is his new home like? Does she like her new school? When will I see him again? Will these sad feelings ever go away?

Most sad feelings do go away, but it may seem like a very long time before they do. Luckily, there are things you can do to make yourself and other people who are missing their families feel better. Talking about your feelings with friends or an adult can help a lot. It may seem like the people around you must know how you feel, but tell them anyway. You may be better at hiding your feelings than you think!

Look around. There are probably many people in your classroom or neighborhood who are missing someone they love. Each of them may have found a different way to feel better about being away from those family members. By talking with other people and sharing your experiences, you'll find out that even when people are far apart geographically, they can still be close in many other ways.

In this book you'll meet a few families and find out why they have to be apart. Then they'll show you some things they do to make their faraway family members seem a little bit closer.

Chapter One

WHEN WE'RE APART

"I promise I'll write to you every day!"

Often when people go away, we make promises like that. But as time goes by, it can get harder and harder to stay in touch. We might forget to write one day, or we might not know what to say in a letter.

One way to keep a promise like that is by writing a letter that's like a diary. Scribble a line or two each day, or whenever you have a special thought or something interesting happens. This is one diary you'll want other people to read! After a few days or weeks, you can mail your letter. Instead of lots of short notes, you'll have one long letter filled with news.

You can even create a secret code to share with just

your faraway friend or family member. Pick certain words or phrases that will have meaning just for you and your pen pal. Or use symbols and numbers to stand for words. You can write each other mystery messages filled with coded news.

Or try writing about your family's times as if you're writing a fairy tale or comic book story: *Once upon a time there was a center fielder named Pat who couldn't catch a fly ball no matter how hard she tried. Then one day, Pat's dad sent her a magic mitt. When she wore the magic mitt (and practiced some more in the backyard with Mom), Pat caught every fly ball.*

P.S. Well, almost every ball.

If you'd rather act than write, use an audiocassette or a video recorder to make a mini-play of things that have happened, then mail it. Act out the roles of your parents, sisters, brothers, teachers, and friends. Will your missing family member guess who's who?

Lots of people keep in touch only once a year, but they do it in a big way. A few of the family members get together and write a newsletter. They include all of the big events in the family for that year — like births, graduations, trips, awards. Then the newsletter is mailed to family and friends far away.

What else can you do to let people know what's happening to you while you're apart? Let a picture tell your story. Keep a diary made up of drawings or photographs instead of words. If sports are a big part of your life, ask someone to take photos of every event in which you compete. Or draw pictures of new people you've met, or of characters from books you've read. Keep a scrapbook you can share with your family later, when you're all together again.

In the following story, Ray is trying to find a way to stay close to his grandmother when his family moves away.

A PROMISE

"Stop swinging, Grandma," Ray scolded. He frowned at his grandmother. "Sit still for just one more minute, okay?"

"Sorry, Ray," Grandma said, looking not a bit sorry. She put out a foot to stop the movement of the porch swing. The chains creaked as she came to a sudden stop. Grandma was still for a moment. Then she started to hum. That wasn't so bad. But when she started to tap her foot and nod her head to the rhythm, Ray groaned.

"Grandma!"

Grandma pretended to freeze in place. She didn't move her head, but spoke out of the corner of her mouth.

"All right, all right. But you know how I hate sitting still."

Ray had to laugh. It was true. Grandma hardly ever sat down for more than a minute. She was always rushing around, visiting friends, volunteering at the hospital where she used to work, taking care of the house, or going to one of many night classes at the local college.

"Okay, one more minute," Ray said. Ray was sitting cross-legged on the floor of the porch. He glanced down at the pad of drawing paper on his lap, then back up at his grandmother. He squinted at her with one eye screwed shut. Grandma tried not to smile.

"The shape of your face is all wrong," Ray said.

Grandma frowned. "You'd better be talking about your sketch, young man," she growled. "And not your model."

"Nope," Ray said, with a teasing grin. He ducked a swipe aimed at the air over his head. Both Ray and his grandma burst out laughing. They were always making each other laugh.

After he stopped giggling, Ray reached for his charcoals. There really was something wrong with Grandma's chin in his sketch. He picked up a piece of lighter-colored charcoal. For the next minute his fingers flew across the page, making changes.

It was because of Grandma that Ray had learned to draw. Grandma had taken a drawing course at the college, and she had brought home the sketch pad and a set of charcoals to practice. One day she had let Ray play with them. After three months Grandma had lost interest in drawing and switched to a course in home repair. But Ray had been hooked. He had been carrying a sketchbook around with him ever since.

"There! It's finished!" Ray ripped the page out of his sketchbook and passed it to his grandmother. She held it up and looked it over carefully. Ray waited, chewing on his lower lip. Ray thought his pictures were getting better and better, but he was always nervous when he showed them to Grandma.

"This is good, Ray, very good," Grandma said in her most serious voice. "I feel like I'm looking in a mirror, only better. You've drawn the real me, not just a reflection of me."

Ray glowed with pride. But the next second his face fell. Grandma passed the picture back to him and said, "I want you to keep this one. Take it with you to Africa to remind you of your old grandma back home."

Africa. Ray's family was leaving next week to spend a year in Tanzania, a country in East Africa. His parents had both gotten jobs teaching English to adults in one of the schools there. For months, Ray's parents had been giving him books about the land, animals, and people he would see in Tanzania. His head was filled with pictures of snow-capped Mount Kilimanjaro, a famous tribe called the Masai, and the grassy Serengeti plains filled with zebras, elephants, lions, and giraffes. All of Ray's friends were jealous. And only a few days ago, Ray had been dying to go.

But two days ago, Ray's mother had told him that Grandma would not be going.

"Somebody needs to stay and watch the house for us," his mother had explained. "And your grandmother has lots of things she wants to do here. She doesn't want to go to Tanzania."

"Not even to be with me? Or with Theola?" Ray had asked in a tiny voice. (Theola was Ray's baby sister.)

Ray's mother had hugged him. "Of course she wants to be with you. It was a hard decision for her to make. But she needs to stay here."

Ray couldn't believe it. He couldn't believe they would leave Grandma behind. She'd be so lonely. Ray felt terrible.

For two days, Ray had been thinking hard. This morning he had come up with an idea. He wouldn't leave Grandma behind. He would stay right here in Illinois, no matter how much he wanted to go to Africa. He would stay behind with Grandma.

So now, when Grandma handed Ray the sketch, Ray remembered his plan. He took a deep breath and announced, "I won't forget you because I'm not going!"

"What do you mean, 'not going'?" Grandma's eyebrows shot up so high and fast Ray thought they'd fly off her head.

"I'm going to stay here with you," Ray said. As soon as he said it, he realized Grandma wouldn't want him to stay if she knew the real reason he was staying. She'd never want him to give up a trip like this one on her account. Ray had to think up another reason. "I don't want to go to Tanzania, anyway. It sounds dumb and boring and..." His voice trailed off. He looked away from his grandmother's bright brown eyes.

"You don't think any such thing," she said. "You've been looking forward to this trip for months!"

Ray thought fast. "But my friends are all here. I won't know anyone."

"You'll make new friends there," said Grandma. "Now, look me right in the eye and tell me the real reason for all this nonsense."

Ray looked her right in the eye. That was his big mistake.

"This is about leaving me here, isn't it?" Grandma said.

Ray hung his head. He should have known she would guess. She always knew how he was feeling.

Grandma took the sketchbook out of Ray's hands. She put it down on the porch and pulled Ray up onto her lap. Usually Ray felt too big for that, but today it was just where he needed to be. Grandma wrapped her arms around his middle and squeezed him tightly.

"I'm going to miss you, too, my little man. Just as much as you'll be missing me," she whispered. "But I'll

10

be thinking of you all the time and that will make you seem close to me. And think how much we'll have to tell each other the next time we're together!"

"But a year's too long. I want to tell you while it's happening! I want you to be there with me!" Ray said.

"That can't happen," Grandma said. "I've got things to do here and you've got things to do there. Who will look after Theola if you stay here with me?"

Ray swallowed hard. He had forgotten about Theola. At home, Ray helped take care of Theola after school while his parents were still at work. She would need her big brother in Tanzania. She would be left all alone if Ray stayed in America.

"I don't know what to do," Ray said.

Grandma thought for a minute. Suddenly she smiled. "I'll tell you what we can do."

"What?" Ray said, twisting around to look her in the face.

"I'll write to you every week, and tell you all the things I'm doing. And all the things the neighbors are doing," Grandma said with a laugh. She liked to gossip. "After all, it will give me something to do in my creative writing class."

Ray laughed, too. He knew in another few months Grandma would be taking some other course, like Filmmaking or Spanish for Beginners. But he also knew she wouldn't forget her promise to write. Maybe she'd send him a video she'd made for class.

"And you can write to me, and tell me all the new things you're discovering," Grandma added.

Ray nodded. But then he thought about how he had promised to write to his friend Lois from summer camp. Somehow, after the first few letters, both of them had just stopped writing.

But Grandma was reading his mind, like always.

"No, I have a better idea," she said. "You draw pictures of all the new things you're seeing in Africa. You save them up and you show them to me when you get back. Then it will be like I was there, but even better, because I'll be seeing it through your eyes." She smiled down at him. "Promise you'll draw me some pictures?"

Ray nodded. That was definitely something he could do. "I promise."

Ray turned around and gave his grandma another hug. He hoped she was reading his mind now — but just in case she couldn't, he said, "I love you, Grandma."

Chapter Two

SHOWING YOU CARE

There are times during the year when you may miss your faraway family even more than usual, especially birthdays, holidays, or when something important happens in your family, town, or school. When you have a big swim meet or a school science fair, you want your family to be there!

It may not seem fair that families can't be together on such special days, but sometimes they have to be apart. Military duty, a job in another state, or long-term travel plans may take family members away for days, weeks, or even months. And even though you know you'll see your relative soon, it might not be soon enough — not in time for a birthday or holiday.

But you can think of ways to bring family members "home" — ways to share the special moments they might miss. Remember, they're probably feeling left out and lonely, too.

In the following story, Susan finds lots of ways to show her sister how much she cares.

A BOX FOR REBECCA

"You are the saddest gummy bear I have ever seen," Mrs. Garber said, looking at the giant-sized piece of candy sitting on the living room couch.

The red gummy bear stuck out her bottom lip. "I can't help it," she said. "I wish Rebecca were here."

The gummy bear was really Susan Garber, wearing her Halloween costume. Susan looked at the pile of candy spread out on the coffee table. On past Halloween nights the sight of all those brightly colored wrappers had her grinning from ear to ear. This year, though, it just made her sigh.

"I've got too many Snickers bars." Susan wrinkled her nose in disgust. "If Rebecca were here, I'd trade them for her Three Musketeers." Rebecca was Susan's older sister, who was away for her first year in college.

"And you'd be fighting over who got stuck with the licorice," Susan's mother reminded her.

Susan shrugged. She could barely remember their fights. All she remembered were the great times she and

Rebecca had once had playing and talking together. Like tonight, for instance, Rebecca should have been around to see Susan's great costume. They had planned it together back in August, right before Rebecca had gone. They always planned Susan's Halloween costume together. Since both sisters loved gummy bears, they had picked that as Susan's costume this year.

"I thought you were tired of having your sister take you trick-or-treating," Susan's mother added. "You said last year it made you feel like a baby. And this year you're nine."

Susan was surprised to hear she had ever felt that way. "Well, this year I miss having her around."

Anyway, walking around alone wasn't the worst part, Susan thought. After all, she had quickly hooked up with her friends Laurel and Marty. It had been fun to go from house to house in a group. But when she got home, Susan had really started missing her sister. Every year, the tradition was for Rebecca and Susan to bargain over the trick-or-treat bags. They would trade and argue over their favorite candies.

This year there was no one trying to snitch Susan's stash of chocolate. There had been no one to make up funny cheers for Susan at the soccer championship game last week, or to tease her about borrowing stuff from Becca's room. Having a sister who was so much older had sometimes been a pain, but most of the time Susan and Becca had been best buddies. Missing a

15

sister was bad enough, but Susan felt like she'd lost her best friend, too. Susan picked up her bag of Halloween candy and dragged her feet up the stairs, even though she still had an hour left until bedtime. Susan's mother looked after her with a worried frown. Then Mrs. Garber suddenly smiled and hurried off to the kitchen.

In her room, Susan stared glumly at her wall calendar. The October page had a cute picture of two kittens climbing on a pumpkin. But not even their furry faces could make her smile. Susan picked up a felt-tip marker and drew a big red X in the box for October thirty-first.

"One...two...three..." Susan counted the days until December 23rd. That was the day Rebecca would come home to Minnesota for Hanukkah and winter break.

"Fifty-two more days," Susan wailed.

"Exactly one day less than when you counted it yesterday," Susan's father said. He was standing in the doorway with Susan's mother.

Susan flung herself on the bed, squashing the back of her puffy gummy costume. She didn't even care. She sighed and stared sadly at the ceiling.

"Before you start moping again, take a look at this," said Susan's mother. She held up a medium-sized cardboard box.

"What's in there?" Susan asked. She struggled to sit up to get a closer look.

"Nothing," Susan's father said. He wiggled his eyebrows and tried to sound mysterious. "Yet."

"I don't get it." Susan looked at her parents like they were crazy.

"This is going to be a care package for your sister," Susan's mother explained. She set the box on Susan's desk.

"We'll fill it with all kinds of stuff. Things that will show Rebecca we care about her," Susan's father added. "Because I bet she's feeling pretty lonely right now."

"Do you think so?" Susan hadn't thought of that. She jumped off the bed and waddled over to her desk. She looked inside the box. "What should we put in it?"

"Well, your mom and I are making Becca's favorite cookies, the ones with nuts."

"Yuck. I hate nuts," Susan said, wrinkling her nose.

"I think that's why your sister likes them," her mother said, "because then you don't eat them all."

"Can I put something in the box?" Susan asked.

Her father nodded. "That's the idea," he said. He started out of the room. "Why don't you think about what you want to send her while we're baking."

"Just don't forget to leave room for the cookies!" Susan's mother warned.

"Sure," Susan said absently. She was already making a list of things to put inside.

Susan's parents were dropping spoonfuls of dough onto two cookie pans when Susan ran into the kitchen a little while later. She was carrying the family's instant camera.

"Mom, could you take my picture?"

"Sure, honey." Susan's mother licked her fingers free of batter, then reached for the camera. "Is this for the box?"

"Yes." Susan struck a silly pose in her gummy bear costume. She was careful not to show the scrunched back part. The camera flash lit up the kitchen.

Susan took the photo when it popped out. "Thanks, Mom!" she said, racing back to her room.

An hour later, Susan's parents reappeared in her bedroom doorway. Susan's father held up two plastic bags filled with cookies. "Did you leave us enough room for these?"

"Just barely," Susan replied. She tilted the box so they could see inside. It was filled almost to the top.

"What have you got in there?" Susan's mother walked over and poked around in the box.

Susan ticked things off on her fingers. "I put in that newspaper with the article about the soccer game last week. You know, the one that said what a good goalie I was," she said. "And I put in my trophy."

"Your soccer trophy?" Susan's father looked impressed. "You're pretty proud of that. Are you sure you want to send it to your sister?"

"Well, she's the one who taught me to play," Susan said. Then she grinned. "Besides, it's only a loan. I put a note on it saying she has to bring it back during winter break."

"What else is in there?" her father asked.

"I took a picture of her room to show her it's just the way she left it."

"That was a good idea," her mother said.

"And I put in a bag of all the Halloween candy she likes. And a note that says she has to send me back some Three Musketeers."

Susan's mother started to laugh. "Becca will feel like she was here for Halloween after all."

"I hope so," Susan said. "Putting together all this stuff for her sort of makes me feel like she's here."

Susan reached up and flipped her calendar page over to November. A kitten was playing in a huge pile of colorful autumn leaves. This time Susan grinned at the furry face in the photograph.

"Can we send another care package to Becca for Thanksgiving?" Susan asked.

"I think that sounds great." Susan's mother moved some stuff around in the box to make room for the bags of cookies. She picked up something that was sitting right on top. It was the photo of Susan posing in her Halloween costume.

"Now this gummy bear looks a lot happier than the one I saw on the sofa," Susan's mother said with a smile.

"She is!" Susan smiled back.

Chapter Three

WILL YOU REMEMBER ME?

When you miss someone, you might wonder, "Does he miss me, too?"

Yes! Just because people move away doesn't mean they stop caring about you. People have to leave their families for all kinds of reasons: they get new jobs, they get married or divorced, or they move to a new house. No matter what the reason for the separation, the feelings you share with people you care about can stay the same even when everything else seems to have changed.

When someone does go away, it can help if you keep a special object that reminds you of them. You can look at the memento and think about the fun things you did together. And you can give the person who's leaving something of yours in return. You'll know that person will think of you whenever he or she sees it.

What kinds of things should you exchange? Find an object that reminds you both of an important place or time you shared. Have a picture taken of the two of you and make two copies. Or give each other copies of your favorite books and sign the first page. You can also make friendship bracelets for one another, sign each other's baseballs, or exchange prized trading cards.

The next story you'll read is about Rico and his family and the special things they share.

TIME TO GO

The rain beat hard against the large window. Rico hoped that the rain would keep falling. He hoped it would rain every day, forever.

"If it keeps raining, they won't let your plane take off," he told his mother.

"Oh, Rico, yes they will." Rico's mother stooped so she could look Rico right in the eye. "Planes take off in all kinds of weather."

"But it's not safe!" Rico said. "How can the pilots see?"

Rico's father smiled reassuringly. "They use radar," he said. "They can 'see' even in the worst storms."

"And they fly way up above the clouds where there

isn't any rain," Rico's mother said. "So don't you worry about me. I'll do all the worrying in this family."

Family. When Rico heard that word he felt his eyes start to burn. Rico turned away to stare out of one of the big airport windows.

Rico's mother and father were getting a divorce. They had told Rico that the two of them couldn't be happy living together anymore. At first, Rico had tried not to believe it. For a while it was easy, because they were all still living together in the big house on Winnona Way.

But now Rico's mother was leaving on one of her business trips on behalf of the bank where she worked. And this time, when she came back from her trip, Rico's mother wouldn't be coming back to the house. Instead, she would be taking Rico with her to a new house in Flagstaff, Arizona. Flagstaff was a whole four-hour drive away from Rico's home in Gallup, New Mexico. Rico would only get to see his father on some weekends and holidays, and during the times his mother was away on one of her trips. Nothing would be like it used to be.

Rico thought of all that while he stared at the runway. "We're not a family anymore," he blurted.

Rico's mother and father looked at each other. Then Rico's mother turned Rico around to face her again.

"That isn't true," she said, looking him straight in the eyes. "We both still love you very, very much and that means we'll always be part of the same family. Because of you."

24

"That's right, mi hijo," said Rico's father. "Like we've been telling you, that's the one thing that will never change."

Rico nodded. They'd been saying the same thing over and over, but it didn't help much.

"Yeah, okay." Rico didn't want to talk about it here. Not here, where he might cry in front of all the people waiting to get on airplanes. He looked around sadly. He wished he could get on a plane and fly away. Far away from all the bad feelings. But that was the problem. His mother was going far away. And when she came back everything would change.

But that wasn't even the worse part. The worse part was that Rico wondered, deep down, if his mother would ever come back. Maybe while she was away she would decide that she didn't love Rico anymore either. When he was with her, Rico knew that those fears were silly. His mother loved him and would love him forever. But now, when she was about to go away, it was easy to get scared.

Rico blinked hard and looked away, out the airport window.

Rico's mother glanced at her watch. She bit her lip in worry. Just then, the loudspeaker blared a message. "Attention passengers for Flight 135. We're sorry, but boarding will be delayed another fifteen minutes. Thank you for your patience."

All around them people groaned and grumbled. But

Rico's mother gave a sigh of relief. "Good. That'll give us a few more minutes to talk."

Behind her, Rico's father cleared his throat. "Why don't I go get us some soda?" Mr. Ruiz said. "Be right back." He headed off toward the busy food cart.

Rico's mother led the way over to some seats in an empty section. Rico was glad. There weren't so many people around them. He was getting tired of holding back his tears.

"We've talked about this before. But we'll talk about it as often as you need to," said Rico's mother.

Rico wasn't listening. He was thinking, if the plane doesn't take off, I'll never have to say good-bye. Mom will just turn around and come back home with us and everything will be like it used to be.

But he knew that wasn't going to happen. He tuned in to his mother's voice again.

"I won't be gone that long, just two months. I'll be back in no time, you'll see," his mother was saying. "And in the meantime, I'll call you and send you postcards with stamps to add to your stamp collection." She touched his nose lightly. "This is just a trip, honey, like all those other trips I've taken. I'll be back."

It's not the same, Rico thought. But he nodded miserably.

"Flight Number 135 now boarding." Rico bit his lip. That was his mother's plane. People pushed and shoved to get on line, but Rico's mother stayed right where she was for another minute.

"I've got to go," she said. "But there's something I want to give you first. It's something very important."

Rico shrugged. What he really wanted was for the plane to drop an engine or something right this minute. Something that would ground it for about a year or so.

Rico's mother put down her suitcase. Maybe I could hide her bag, Rico thought. Then she couldn't leave.

But then Rico noticed what his mother was doing. She had pushed up her sleeve and was unbuckling the watch on her right wrist.

"I want you to have this."

Rico took the old watch, staring down in disbelief. "Abuelo's watch. For me?"

"Yes, your grandfather's watch." Rico's mother took the watch and buckled it around his wrist. She had to use the last hole on the watchband.

"You take care of this while I'm away," Rico's mother told him. "It will remind you I'll be thinking of you every hour of every day."

Rico stroked the old watch. It was made of silver, with turquoise stones around the sides. It was tarnished now, but still beautiful. It had a strong square face, just like the grandfather Rico knew only from photographs.

This was his mother's most cherished belonging.

"What if I lose it?" Rico asked. He pressed his hand down on the watch protectively.

"I know you'll take good care of it," his mother said.

"But even if you did lose it, it wouldn't matter. I'd think of you anyway and love you just the same."

"No matter what?"

"No matter what. And no matter where I am."

Looking down at the watch, Rico knew his mother would be back. She would never leave behind her most prized possession. "Thanks, Mom," Rico said. He was blinking very fast now.

"I love you, honey." She hugged him fiercely.

"I love you too, Mom."

"You'd better run, Luz," said a voice behind them. It was Rico's father, holding two cups of soda. "Your plane is about to take off."

"Ay, Dios mío!" Rico's mother gave him a quick kiss. Then she ran over to the gate. Rico watched as she handed over her ticket and began to walk away with a wave.

"Mom! Mom!"

Rico raced over.

"You forgot your suitcase!"

Chapter Four

FAMILY PHOTOS

Have you ever looked at a family photo and asked, "Who's that?" Most people have relatives they've never even met before. It may be strange for you to know there are family members out there whom you've never seen.

These faraway family members may not be able to visit for months or even years, if ever.

That doesn't mean you can't get to know them, at least a little bit. You'll feel closer to your family when you find out more about them. Ask the family members you do see what they remember about other relatives you've never seen. Sometimes it's easier to get to "know" people if you look at pictures of them as you listen to stories.

Are there things in your home that have been passed along from one generation to the next? Maybe it's not even an object, but a saying, a lullaby, or a family name.

In the next story, learning more about her family helps Surya feel closer to her people in distant India.

FOOTSTEPS TOWARD FAMILY

Thump-thump-thump-thump.

Surya watched the elderly man's hand move the wooden pachisi piece across the board.

"Uh-oh," said Surya's best friend, Rajesh. Surya groaned when she saw where the piece would land.

Thump-thump.

"Grandfather wins again," Rajesh said, trying not to grin. It was the third game in a row Surya had lost to Mr. Bhatt.

Rajesh's grandfather shook the dice in his thin hands. He smiled at Surya and raised one eyebrow inquisitively.

"No way!" Surya said, shaking her head and smiling. "I've lost enough today, thanks. Besides, I've got to get home."

Surya waited while Rajesh told his grandfather there was no time for another game. She wished she could understand Gujarati like her friend, but Surya's parents only spoke English at home. Besides, the Indian language her family knew was Hindi, not Gujarati.

As she walked home that afternoon, Surya thought hard about the day she had spent with Rajesh and his grandparents.

Surya used to be glad her parents didn't make her wear the long, wrapped dresses called saris, speak Hindi, or say prayers each morning as more traditional Indians do. Some of the other kids in her school got teased for being different. But lately Surya felt she wanted to know more about her family history. She wanted to know more about being Indian.

That night at dinner, Surya just picked at her chicken curry. That was one thing, at least, she knew about her family in India. They had a wonderful recipe for spicy curry powder!

Surya made a smooth round pile out of her basmati rice.

"That's neat, Surya. Is it a snowman?" said Surya's little brother, Rama. Surya was eight, two years older than Rama.

Rama grabbed his spoon and started piling his own rice into a lumpy tower.

"Stop playing with your food, you two," said Surya's mother. Then she looked more closely at Surya's serious face. "Is anything wrong, little one?"

"Rajesh's grandma and grandpa were at his house today."

"Yes? And so?"

"So where are my grandparents?" Surya asked. "How come they never come and visit me? Don't they care about me?"

Surya's mother looked shocked. "Of course they care! They love you."

"Me, too?" Rama asked. His rice tower fell over.

"You, too."

Across the table, Surya's father set down his fork. He looked serious, too. "Your grandparents are in India, Surya. You know that. India is far away. It's too expensive for them to travel that distance."

"But I want to see them!" Surya said.

"Me, too!" said Rama.

"I want to see them, too," said Surya's mother. "Remember, they are my mother and father, as well as your grandparents." Surya was surprised to see tears in her mother's eyes.

"And my mother is still there," said Surya's father. "My sister and her family, too."

"And my two brothers," her mother added.

Surya hadn't even thought about that. Of course her parents missed their families, even more than Surya did. She couldn't imagine being that far from her own parents. And even though Rama could be a pest sometimes, she'd hate being even one mile away from him. India was thousands of miles away from North Carolina.

"We're saving so that one day we can all go back to India to visit our family," said Surya's mother. "We want you to meet everyone. Not just your grandparents, but your uncles, aunts, and cousins, as well."

Surya tried to remember the photos in the family album. But it had been a while since she'd looked at it, and the last time, she hadn't paid much attention. It had seemed boring then. But now, she tried to imagine a whole family that she had never seen. In her mind all the aunts looked like her mom and all the uncles looked like her dad. In Surya's mind, all her cousins looked like Rama, except the girls had long black braids. That made her giggle.

Rama giggled, too.

Surya felt a little bit better. But she still had lots of questions.

"What are they like?"

"We've told you stories about our family many times," her mother reminded her.

"And you have seen their pictures," her father added.

"I wish I knew what they were really like," Surya sighed.

Surya's mother said, "I can think of something that might help." She smiled at Surya's father. "The tabla."

"Of course!" He pushed back his chair and left the

kitchen.

"What's a tabla?" Surya asked.

"You'll see," said her mother. "Now let's clear these plates and go into the living room."

When Surya's father reappeared, the rest of the family was sitting on the couch in the living room. They were looking at the photo album.

"And this is your father's mother. She's your grandmother Anand," Surya's mother was saying.

Surya looked down at a photo she had seen before. A tall woman with a long, thin face stood against a white wall. She wore a sari in the colors of the sea, shot with silver. Surya touched her own short black hair as she looked at the woman in the picture. Surya loved her own haircut, but she thought Anand's long hair was very pretty.

Surya's father leaned over and put something on the coffee table. "Your grandmother gave this tabla to me when I was your age," he said.

"Drums!" Surya was surprised. Her father had played bongo drums?

Then Surya looked more closely at the set of two drums. They weren't bongos. One of the drums was smaller and made of wood. The larger one was made of shiny metal.

"My mother — your grandmother Anand — is the best tabla player in the whole state of Punjab," Surya's father said. She could hear the pride in his voice.

34

"I've heard her play. She is wonderful," said Surya's mother. "She can sing as sweetly as a bird, too. She knows many ragas."

Surya pointed to the stack of cassettes near the stereo. "Ragas? You mean those songs on your tapes?"

Her father nodded. "My mother taught me how to play when I was just a boy." He sat beside the coffee table and tapped the drums lightly.

Brummmm. Brummmmm.

Then he placed his left hand on the bigger drum and began to beat out a rhythm with his palm.

"Sa Re Ga Ma Pa Da Ni," sang Surya's mother softly. She was keeping the rhythm by slapping her hand against her leg. First she hit with her palm, then with the back of her hand. Back and forth, back and forth.

Surya listened for a minute. Then she reached out and touched the metal drum with a fingertip.

"May I play?" she asked.

"Me, too. Can I play?" Rama shouted, bouncing up and down on the sofa.

"No, Rama. These are for Surya," Surya's father said gently. "When you were born, Surya, your grandmother told me she wanted you to have this tabla. It was her favorite."

He lifted the tabla and looked at it a moment with a faraway look in his eyes. Then he handed the drums to Surya, placing them carefully in her hands. "My mother told me to give this to you when you were old enough to understand how important a gift it is."

"I understand," said Surya. She felt as if her grandmother herself were really handing her the drums. Surya banged her palm gently against one side and listened to its music.

"Our family in India is very far away," said Surya's father. "But these drums, and the stories we tell about them, are like a rope. A rope that joins you to your people and homeland no matter where they are and no matter where you are."

Surya nodded. But to her, the tabla did not seem like

a rope. Instead, when she listened to its music, each beat of the drums was like a footstep. Each beat brought her closer and closer to the family she had never seen.

"I'll learn how to play. Someday, I'll go to India and play for my grandmother," Surya promised, as she beat on the drums, "and for my aunts and uncles and all my cousins."

"Me, too!" shouted Rama.

Brummmmm. Brummmmmm.

Chapter Five

WHAT'S NEW? EVERYTHING!

Sometimes you're the one who is going far away from your family. How does that feel?

It can be very exciting, but usually it feels lonely at first. Leaving behind the people and places you're familiar with is never easy. When your family has been an important part of your life, moving away from them can feel like a part of you has been taken away. That's not really what happens, though. Your family is something you take with you wherever you go.

Nowadays there are lots of ways to stay close to family and friends — letters, phone calls, home videos, even computer bulletin boards. Family reunions are one way for everyone to get together at the same time.

But just as important as staying close to your family is finding a new "family" in the place where you live. Making new friends doesn't mean that you have to get rid of your old friends and family. There's a place for everyone! Sharing stories of your far-off family with new friends is fun. Soon, you'll be able to tell your faraway family stories about adventures with your new friends.

In the next story, Mike finds a way to feel better about moving to a new place.

ONE SPECIAL DAY

Mike made a list:

Things I hate about moving to Seattle:

1 - leaving Aunt Trac, Uncle Paul, and cousin Tuan

2 - leaving my friends, especially Tim and Chris

3 - changing school halfway through the year

4 - the weather, which is always cold and gray and wet

Mike wrote the list on a page from his math notebook. When he was done, he taped it to the mirror in his bedroom. Then he sat on the bed and stared at his fish tank. That was the only good thing about the move to Seattle, Mike thought. Now that he had his own room, and didn't have to share with Tuan, there was enough space for things like a fish tank.

"I've only been here two weeks and already I hate it," Mike told his bug-eyed goldfish, Fred. "No offense, Fred, but I'd even trade you to go back home." Mike was sure he'd always think of California as home.

There was a knock on Mike's door. His mother opened it a split second before he yelled, "Come in!"

She poked her head around the edge of the door. "Chào," Mrs. Nguyen said, a happy "hello." "And how was your day *tôm?*"

Even when Mike was in a bad mood, he had to smile whenever his mother called him *tôm*. Mike would accuse his mother of forgetting his name. Mrs. Nguyen insisted that she was calling him *tôm*, Vietnamese for a shrimp, because he was small for his age and liked to hide in his "shell." It was a special joke, just between the two of them.

"My name isn't *tôm*," Mike reminded his mother, just as he always did.

"Okay, okay," she said with a grin. "So, how was your day?"

"Terrible," Mike said. His smile quickly disappeared. "Just like yesterday and the day before."

"Well, I had a very nice day," Mike's mother said. "It's so good to be working with numbers again." Mrs. Nguyen was the new accountant for a chain of Italian restaurants. Her job was the reason they had moved to Seattle. "It's much better for me than working in that restaurant or the clothing shop," she added with a roll of her eyes.

Mike had to smile again. His mother had been a bad salesclerk and an even worse waitress. At the store, she told customers not to buy clothes she thought were ugly. Her boss didn't like that very much. And at the restaurant, she was always dropping things off serving trays — usually onto a customer's head or lap! But those had been the only jobs she could find after she had been laid off from her job in a big computer company last year.

There were no other accounting jobs in the small town in California where they had lived. And they really needed the money. Mike's father had died right after he was born, and Mike and his mother had moved in with her sister's family. So when Mike's mother lost her job, they at least had a home with Mike's aunt and uncle. But they still needed food, a car, and the clothes that Mike was growing out of a mile a minute.

When a friend called to offer Mike's mother a job in Seattle, she had jumped at the chance. Unfortunately for Mike, it felt like a leap off the side of a cliff.

"Today I finished cleaning up the ledgers," his mother said. "Now I can start with my own system. I'll have it running like a clock in no time."

She was about to say something else when she saw Mike's list taped to the mirror. Mike watched as she read it. He felt bad when he saw his mother's smile fade into a frown.

"Do you really hate it here so much?"

"Yes," Mike said, picking at his bedspread. "I miss everybody back home and nobody at school is nice to me. I know I'm never going to make friends. I'm behind in all my subjects and I don't like my teachers and I just hate going to school every day." Mike finished with a sigh.

"You've always liked school," his mother said.

"Not now that I'm the 'new kid.' I'm tired of everything being different and being so far away from everyone we know," Mike said in a rush, "and there are practically no more holidays before spring vacation and it's ages until we can go back to California to visit."

"We'll be there for Thanh Minh." Mike's mother reminded him about the celebration honoring their ancestors. During Thanh Minh, Vietnamese people visit the graves of family members and bring offerings of paper money and food. It was a time to think about the special ways families are connected through generations. When Mike was old enough to realize what they were doing he was a little spooked at first. Lately, though, he had started to like those yearly visits, especially visiting his father's grave. It was one of the only times he felt close to the father he had never known.

Thinking about the festival didn't help now, though. "Thanh Minh isn't until April," Mike groaned. The way he said it made it sound like years instead of a few months.

Mike flopped over on the bed and hid his face in the pillow. "I wish I could just stay in my room until June and start school in the fall when everyone's new," he said in a muffled voice.

Mike's mother stroked his hair gently. She was thinking. "I have an idea," she said.

Mike rolled over. "Do I get to stay home?" he joked.

"Yes."

"What?" Mike shook his head. I must be hearing things, he thought.

His mother just laughed and held up one finger.

"One day. You can stay home one day before spring vacation. If you get up in the morning and it seems like you just can't stand it that day, you can stay home. I'll stay home, too. We can spend the day together exploring this cold, wet, gray city you hate so much."

Just then the sun came out. They both started laughing.

"We'll call it..." Mike's mother tapped her chin, "...our Red-Letter Day." Red was a lucky color in Vietnam, Mike knew. And here in America a "red-letter day" meant a very special day. It was the perfect name.

"Any day?" Mike said. "Tomorrow? Could I take it tomorrow?"

Mike's mother frowned. "It would be hard for me to take a day off so soon." Then she saw his face fall. "But yes, if you want."

Mike thought a minute. "Well, maybe not tomorrow. I mean, tomorrow we have basketball tryouts."

"Well, you think about it. And any day you just can't take it anymore, you tell me in the morning and I'll give my boss a call."

She tugged his arm. "Now help me get dinner."

———

The next morning, Mike woke up feeling lonely. He missed Tuan most in the morning, when they used to joke with each other as they got ready for school. He looked sadly out at the cloudy morning. "Maybe I'll take my Red-Letter Day today after all," Mike said to himself.

But then he remembered basketball tryouts.

So Mike dragged himself to school. That afternoon in gym class, a girl named Tisha showed Mike a new steal. Mike used it during tryouts and made the team. Tisha made the team, too, using some tips Mike had taught her.

Mike thought about the Red-Letter Day every morning when he woke up. Each morning he thought, "Maybe today." Then he would think, "What if it gets worse? I'd better wait." But every day it got a little bit better.

There was a whole week when he missed Tuan, Aunt Trac, and Uncle Paul so much he felt his heart would break. But Mike's mother let him call California. He talked for a whole hour, even though it was long-distance. And then the next day he needed to go to school to tell Tisha and his other new friend, Rob, about how his cousin Tuan had gotten the lead in the class play. And how Tuan had knocked over the whole set during the big musical number.

Then Chris sent Mike a great hologram postcard, which he took to school the next day to show to all his new friends.

It seemed like there was something important to do every day for the next few weeks — an art contest one day, a big math test or a hockey game at recess the next. A month went by, then another. Suddenly, spring vacation was only two weeks away.

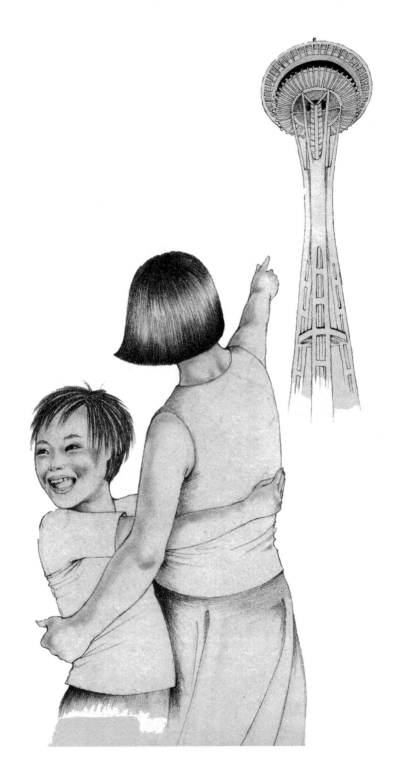

"Pretty soon we'll see Trac, Paul, and Tuan," Mike's mother said one morning at breakfast as she shook cereal into two bowls.

Mike nodded happily. He was surprised to realize that thinking about his family and friends far away didn't hurt so much anymore. He still missed everyone, but he could laugh with his new friends, too. And his mother's boss — the friend who had offered her the job — was like another aunt to Mike. Things weren't so bad in Seattle after all.

"Hey! I just realized something," Mike said through a mouthful of cereal. "I never took my Red-Letter Day."

"So you noticed, hmm?" his mother said. "And don't talk with your mouth full."

Mike swallowed hard. "I guess I didn't need it as much as I thought I would," Mike said. "But I wish I had taken it anyway, just for fun."

Mike's mother looked out the kitchen window at the bright sunny day. Then she grinned.

"Why don't we take it today?" she said. "We can change the rules a little. We'll use it to celebrate instead."

"Excellent!" Mike jumped out of his chair. "It really is my lucky day!"

Activities

YOUR FAMILY TREE

Who's who in your family? Do you know the names of all your grandparents, aunts, uncles, and second-cousins-once-removed?

It can be difficult to keep track of all those cheek-pinching relatives, but it's easier to feel connected to faraway family when you know where they belong on your family tree. It's nice to know where you belong, too.

A family tree is a record of all the people in your family. Your tree has roots and branches just like a living tree. The roots are the earliest family members you can find. The roots of your tree might be your grandparents. Some families can trace their roots back to great-great-great-great grandparents, or even farther!

From your family's roots, lots of branches may grow. A brother may marry. His wife's family can be added to your tree. You're part of her family now, too. An aunt's new baby can be added, because he's your new cousin.

Of course, family trees can get pretty crowded. Once you get into second cousins (your cousin's kids) or great-grandparents (your grandparents' parents), things can get complicated!

Here's an example of a simple family tree:

PICTURE A

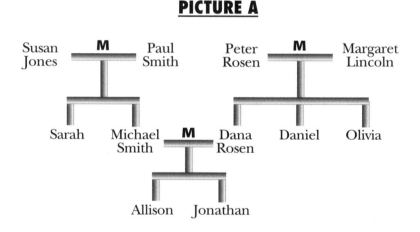

Can you see how new branches might be formed? What would happen if Allison married and had two children? Picture B on the next page shows how you would add new people.

PICTURE B

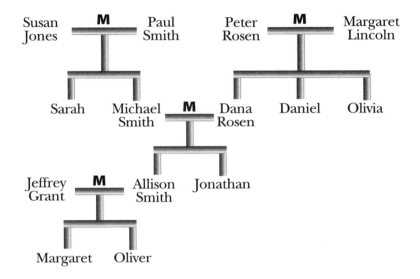

How many branches of your family tree can you trace? Probably more than you think. Ask people in your family about relatives they remember. Find out as much specific information as you can. Collect photographs of all your family members to use to decorate your family tree.

Here is a form you can use when you interview family members. After you've finished a form like this for every person you learn about, you can start creating your own family tree.

FAMILY FACT FINDING FORM

RELATIVE'S NAME	NICKNAME

BORN (WHEN/WHERE):

DIED (WHEN/WHERE):

FATHER'S NAME	FATHER'S NICKNAME
MOTHER'S NAME	MOTHER'S NICKNAME

MARRIED TO/ON(MONTH/DAY/YEAR)/BY:

Children (Oldest to youngest)	BORN MONTH/DAY/YEAR	DIED MONTH/DAY/YEAR	MARRIED TO.	MARRIED ON MONTH/DAY/YEAR
1				
2				
3				
4				
5				

FUN FACTS OR STORIES ABOUT MY RELATIVE

It can be hard work making a family tree. But when you record your family's roots and branches, you'll be leaving a record for the kids who come after you. Your great-great-granddaughter may be filling in the branches of your family tree in the year 2100!

If you can answer only a few of these questions for each relative, that's okay. The farther back you go in your family tree, the harder it may be to find the facts. Just write down whatever you learn and keep asking those questions. Who knows what you might find out? Maybe your grandfather rode in a posse. Perhaps a cousin invented the zipper. Maybe an ancestor took the first photograph! You never know until you ask.

Jung Family Photograph: Collection, Balch Institute for Ethnic Studies

Scott-Johnson Family Photograph: Collection, Balch Institute for Ethnic Studies

SHOW-YOU-CARE PACKAGE

There are times family members miss each other even more than usual — birthdays, holidays, even reunions. But no matter how far apart you are, those days can still be days your whole family can share. Just send a little bit of that special day to faraway relatives — in a care package.

You can put anything in a care package. Try to think of things that will make faraway family members feel like they were with you that day. You don't even have to wait for a special day. Care packages are fun to pack — and fun to open — any time.

Here are some ideas for things to put in your care package:

- a local newspaper

- a photo of yourself that you've had taken since you

said good-bye. Or tape together several big sheets of construction paper. Ask an adult to trace your outline while you lie on the paper. Then you can fill in the outline with a drawing of yourself. Or use the space to paste in a collage of pictures, words, and other objects that relate to you. Be sure to add notes about how you've changed since you last saw each other: describe a new haircut or outfit, or how many inches you've grown.

- something to help celebrate the special day: balloons, party hats, and horns for a birthday; Valentine candy hearts; an April Fools' Day trick; or something to celebrate a religious holiday.

- photographs of familiar things at home, or things that have changed around the house or town.

- a favorite food (pack those eggs very carefully!), or a recipe for a food that's a new favorite.

- a tape recording of each family member sending a message. Remember to let any pets add messages, too. (Let your family and friends think about what they want to say first. You won't get so many "ums.")

- a small gift that means something special to the two of you. A good gift is a supply of pre stamped postcards for sending messages back home. You can buy them at the post office. Get some for yourself, too. That way you can just scribble a quick note or drawing whenever you get the urge.

Can you think of things you'd like to send to someone far away?

GLOSSARY

basmati
rice

chào
greeting in Vietnamese

Dios mío
my God

Gujarati
the language of Gujarat and neighboring regions in northwestern India

Hanukkah
an eight-day Jewish holiday commemorating rededication of the Temple of Jerusalem

Hindi
a literary and official language of northern India

hologram
a three-dimensional picture that is made without the use of a camera

Masai
members of a pastoral and hunting people of Kenya and Tanzania

mi hijo
my child

pachisi
an ancient board game played with dice and counters on a cruciform board in which players attempt to be the first to reach the home square

pen pal
a friend made and kept through correspondence

raga
one of the ancient traditional melodic patterns
or modes in Indian music

sari
a garment worn by southern Asian women that
consists of several yards of lightweight cloth draped
so that one end forms a skirt or pajama and the
other a head or shoulder covering

Serengeti
a national park in Tanzania. The Serengeti is a dry
treeless plain over which millions of wildebeest and
gazelle migrate each year during the rainy season.
Lions, giraffes, zebras, hippos, and many other
animals also live on the Serengeti.

tabla
a pair of small different-sized hand drums used
especially in Indian music

Thanh Minh
a celebration in Vietnam honoring ancestors that is
somewhat comparable to U.S. Memorial Day

tôm
shrimp in Vietnamese